Leave It to

By Rita Golden Gelman

Pictures by Mort Gerberg

SCHOLASTIC INC.

New York   Toronto   London   Auckland   Sydney

ISBN 0-590-33642-8

Text copyright © 1987 by S&R Gelman Associates, Inc.
Illustrations copyright © 1987 by Mort Gerberg.
Art direction by Diana Hrisinko.
Text design by Theresa Fitzgerald.
All rights reserved. Published by Scholastic Inc.
HELLO READER is a trademark of Scholastic Inc.

12 11 10 9 8 7 6 5 4 3   0 1 2 3/9

Printed in the U.S.A.   08
First Scholastic printing, March 1987

For the Davis Family...
so others may laugh
because Jessica did.
                    —R.G.G.

For Aaron...
and Diane, and Alan, too.
                    —M.G.

"This is fun.

This is great.

I'm jumping.

I'm flipping."

"Oh, no!" shouted Minnie.

"You're dumping.

You're dripping."

"Plug up the hole with your finger,"
she said.

"That soda is spilling all over
the bed."

So he plugged up the hole.

And he started to flip.

He jumped.

And he flopped.

Then he stopped for a sip.

"Oh, no. Minnie, look!

Oh, no.

What bad luck!

I can't sip the soda.

My finger is stuck!"

"Don't worry," said Minnie.

"Just leave it to me.

That finger is nothing.

Hmmmmm.

Let me see."

"First I'll tie you all up.

Then I'll tie me to you.

That thing will come off.

I know just what to do."

"See," Minnie said.

"I knew I could do it!"

"But look at that window.

The bottle went through it!"

"Don't worry," said Minnie.

"Just leave it to me.

That window is nothing.

Hmmmmm.

Let me see."

"I'll glue up the glass.

I'll put on a lot.

Then I'll stick up this picture

right over the spot."

"I love it.

I do.

Even more than before.

But look at the glue.

It's all over the floor."

"Don't worry," said Minnie.

"Just leave it to me.

A glue-mess is nothing.

Hmmmmm.

Let me see."

"The best cleaner-upper,

as everyone knows,

is water.

Watch out!

Here I come with the hose!"

"See, glue was no problem.

No problem, I say.

I squirted the water

and washed it away!"

"But, Minnie,
I don't think we're finished.
Not yet!

The glue is all gone,

but the house is all wet!"

"Don't worry," said Minnie.

"Just leave it to me.

A wet house is nothing.

Hmmmmm.

Let me see."

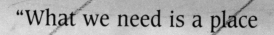

"What we need is a place
for the water to go.

I will make one right now.

Watch out for your toe!"

"I love you, I do,

even more than before.

But what will we do

with this hole in the floor?"

"A hole in the floor
is nothing,
I say.

I knew I could do it.
Now we can play."

"We can bounce.

We can bump.

We can jump on the bed.

We can fly.

We can flip.

We can flop,"

Minnie said.

"Freddy,

come on.

Let's do it.

Let's go."

"As soon

as I

plug up this

hole with my toe."

"Oh. No."